Did I hear
   someone sobbing
where in the tranquil universe
   did it come from

The Purple Ribbon
紫色絲帶

Eric S. Mak

我聽到一陣
　　哭泣聲嗎
在寧靜的宇宙
那裡來的呢

Tellwell Talent
www.tellwell.ca

ISBN
978-0-2288-3389-5 (Hardcover)
978-0-2288-3390-1 (Paperback)
978-0-2288-3388-8 (eBook)

乘風飄翔

上天空

每片葉胎带

我对他的思念

与掛懷

往尋覓他

up with the wind

into the sky

every single leaf

carries my thoughts and

emotions of him

   going to find him

紅　葉

仰向遊云
俯視池澤
叢林

掠过狂風
密雨

跟隨溪流
蕩漾汪洋中

小魚向我眨眨眼
陪伴我

A Red Leaf

asking the clouds

looking down at the swamps

and jungles

sweeping through the storms

and rain

following the streams

flowing in the ocean

little fish blink at me

accompany me

不論你在你的地方

何處

也許一天

落葉片片

你望向

夕陽

想起一女孩

那回你手接

樹上飄下

一片紅葉

給于她

遠遠的地方

很久很久以前

wherever you are

in your place

perhaps one day

leaves floating in the wind

you look to

the evening sky

and think of a girl

you once caught

a red leaf

falling from a tree

gave it to her

a far far place

long long ago

直至那時
太陽晦暗
沒有樹木
鳥兒
山嶺風化
成沙末
海洋乾涸
至深底

無風
沉寂寂
而在那
地球的邊緣
天際的盡處
一小葉
輕輕的
向他落下

                    until the time
        the sun is dull
        no trees
        no birds
                    mountains have eroded
        into sand
                    oceans have dried up
        to the bottom
                    windless
                    calm
                            and there
        at the edge of earth
        end of the sky
                    one little leaf
        slowly falling down
        to him

当你看到
一片红叶
在你手里
残破沧桑
泪水满溢
它的眼睛

向着你微笑
你可认识它
及记得
那时移世易
的女孩吗

12

when you see

a red leaf

in your hand

torn and faded

    tears swell up

in its eyes

    smiling at you

would you recognize it

and remember

    the girl

from the past world

我終于找到你
憩息在你
安全溫暖掌心裏
凝望你
多一次

輕撫你的手
低声説再會
合上眼
枯萎而去
留下你在
無際空洞的世界
孤零一人

I finally found you

resting in your

warm and safe palm

looking up at you

one more time

touching your hand

quietly saying goodbye

I close my eyes

withering

leaving you behind

in this vast and empty world

all alone

I will miss you

wherever

I will be

可不知道
我會在那處
如能讓我
想著妳

17

我將往

攀登懸崖

鷹鳥嚇去

採摘她最喜歡的

野莓子

最後一次

I shall go

      climbing the cliffs

eagle scared away

picking the wild berries

she likes

      my last time

如果妳要我離去人世間

我再不會与妳
海濱競跑
海鷗上空飛翔
海浪在我们身旁捲動
妳的秀髮
在我面前飄蕩
妳快樂的
欢笑声

If you want me to die

I shall no longer

race you down the beach

seagulls flying above

waves rolling beside us

your hair waving

in front of me

your joyous voice

laughing aloud

我將不看到妳

晴天下

海洋清風中

牽着妳未來

孩子的手

海岸漫步

拾貝殼

I shall not see you

under sunny skies

in the ocean breeze

holding the hands of

   your future children

strolling on the seashore

   picking seashells

如我是一
　蜻蜓
歇息在妳的窗框上
窺視妳
早晨起來
伸展妳的臂膀

化妝檯前
梳理妳的長髮
留下一
粉紅色菊花
悄悄離去

24

If I should be

a dragonfly

　　resting on your windowpane

peeping at you

　　as you awaken to morning light

stretch your arms

　　and comb your hair

in front of your vanity

　　I would leave you

a pink daisy

　　quietly fly away

或是一蜜蜂

繞着妳營營的

当妳在後園

摘苣时

追我

像往昔的

妳可忍心

拍傷我嗎

瞇着眼：

妳看到我

此时是

那么的弱小嗎

26

or a bee

buzzing around you

while you pick peas

in your garden

    chase me

as in the past

    do you really want

to harm me

    my eyes blinking

"do you see

    now that

I am so tiny"

又或是一小魚

在池塘

咬嚙妳的足趾

急速游去

在妳呼喝

猛力踢水時

回頭

凝眼望向妳：

「難道妳看不到

那是我嗎

？」

28

or else a little fish

nipping at you toe

in the pond

flitting away

when you yelp

kicking the water hard

looking back

in my wet eyes

"would you not see

  it is me"

更又或是

一陣南風

輕柔地吹

撫著妳

妳可聽到我

等著妳

藏在我心底處

在我

吹過萬山嶺

橫越海洋

羽

30

or yet

a southern wind

gently blowing on you

    caressing you

would you hear me

carrying you with me

    deep in me

when I sweep

through the mountains

across the oceans

而有一天
晚餐後

妳想
往外邊散步

披上妳的外套
關上後門

腳踏厚厚的黃葉
沿著光禿的樹走

32

maybe one day

after supper

you feel like

going for a walk outside

you put on your sweater

close the door

step on the thick yellow leaves

walk along the bare trees

冷風吹

妳抱緊自身

望上

秋日晚霞

想著一男孩

那夕妳告訴他

妳不要再看到他

妳要他

消失他自己

a chilly wind blows

you hold yourself tight

looking up

to autumn's sunset sky

you think of the boy

you told him that evening

you didn't want to see him

you asked him

to make himself disappear

妳看到他
抹着眼
放下一袋
橘紅菓子
走入山林
回頭望妳
消失在妳的
視線

那夕如今夕
長空陰鬱
風呼号
樹葉吹蕩
很多很多年前

you saw him

wipe his eyes

put down a bag of

    ripe berries

running into the woods

a look back at you

vanished from

    your eyesight

    it was like this evening

the sky was gloomy

wind howling

yellow leaves falling

    many many years ago

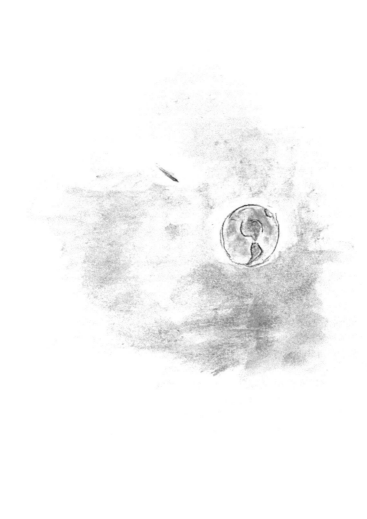

妳會看我
　一眼嗎

妳可注意到

我在那裏嗎

40

will she

have a glance at me

will she notice

I am there

来自宇宙一火星

如果你看到一火星
自宇宙到来
请不要
告诉我

或那火星不曾到来
宇宙如往昔的
宁静如斯
也请别
告我知

42

A Spark from the universe

if there came a spark

from the universe

do not

let me know

or if the spark never came

the universe is as usual

calm and peaceful

also do not

let me know

我將不知道

她曾到來

或沒有

也許她已

回家去了

遠遠的星系

44

I will not know

if she has come

or not

or she may have

returned home

to a far away galaxy

浮游在太空裏

幻夢着她

她金黄的髮絲

穿过

点点凡星

她高声的欢笑

横越太空

惊醒

夢中的宇宙

floating in space

in my dream of her

her golden hair

weaving

between the stars

her loud laughter

sweeping through space

awakening the universe

asleep

外边
常有火星
劃过
每次一火星
经近我时
我抬头
想着
那可會是她

48

sparks

shooting

above

every time there is one

passing by

I would rise

wondering if

it was her

但願那一天
跳上一東近的
彗星
在後面追趕
星系又星系
我能終于
追上她嗎

50

may one day

jumping on a comet

coming by

going behind her

    galaxy after galaxy

will I ever be able to

catch up to her

只要一天
她回頭
向我一微笑

52

if only one day

she would look back

a smile

at me

leaving home

will I be back

別了家

我會回來嗎

太空一石塊

很多彗星劃过

很多星星經过

在太空一直前往

無止境

56

A stone in Space

many comets going by

passing many many stars

soaring in space

endlessly

直至那一天
出宇宙
脱我的困禁
抵达那境域
从不曾
有人知道
有人达至

Until when

I can be out of the universe

free from my boundary

reaching where

no one

    has ever known

      ever been

如我落下
你的行星

為一男孩
驚訝的注視妳

好奇地觸著妳的秀髮

從妳處
學習妳的語言

同享一雪糕
勾妳一起上學堂

一同成長
量度我们的身高

60

if I would descend

on your planet

as a child

    astonishingly staring at you

    curiously touching your hair

    learning your language

     from you

    sharing an ice cream

    walking to school with you

    growing together

    measuring our heights

沿着小溪跑
從石頭跳上
另一塊
妳跪低
手觸清涼流水
一孤葉
順水流下

「看 她可會是那
紅葉女孩嗎
她看似很辛勞及沉默
她可遠程
歷盡滄桑了
我希望她安好
祝她好運」

running along a stream

leaping from rock

to rock

you kneel down

to feel the cool water

a lone leaf

flowing by

"look   could it be that

red leaf girl

she looks so weary and quiet

she must have come

a long long way

I hope she is fine

I wish her good luck"

攀登洛磯峰

我眼睛射光

追走野狼

高風吹

給她披上

我的外衣

手觸云朵

給她指向

我來自藍天

後面

64

climbing the Rockies

my eyes beam

turning away the wolves

    alpine wind blowing

putting my jacket

on her

    touching the clouds

showing her

behind the blue sky

I came from

直至我該離去

的時候

將她從蘋菓樹上

放下

凝視她

多一次

我會再見到

她嗎

也許

在宇宙遠深處

我以外

她雙臂展開

向着我興奮欢笑

Until the time

I should leave

> *putting her down*

from the apple tree

> *gazing at her*

one more time

> *will I ever*

see her again

> *maybe*

in the far universe

or beyond

> *her arms open to me*

laughing joyously

「你冷嗎

　　餓嗎

你看到我穿上

你的外衣嗎

你何不

多拿些蘋菓

遠行呢」

68

"are you cold

    are you hungry

do you see me

with you jacket on

    why didn't you take

some more apples with you

for your journey"

「你翩廷太空到來

投下在

我平靜的心湖

漣漪起伏

一個跟一個

你何不僅只

經過而往

從不進入

我的生命呢」

70

"you came through space

hitting on the peaceful pond

of my heart

ripples spreading out

one after another

shouldn't you have just

gone by and left

having never entered

my life"

「不論你往你的地方

現在何處

如我能是

一小星星

照亮

你的行程」

72

"wherever you are going

for your goals

if I could be

a little star

lighting

your way"

長髮　　唯望那一天　　別矣　　so long
我是妳的　　　　　　　　　　　　may someday

I could be your

long hair

我去了
我將不再
煩擾妳
我會
想著妳在我
離去這世界的時刻

我希望是
妳的長髮
貼附著妳
常與妳一起

I shall be gone

not annoying you

    anymore

I shall be

thinking of you

    as I leave the world

I wish to be

your long hair

attached to you

    always with you

長髮

如妳偶爾
想想
我们过往的时日
朦朧細雨下漫步
細雨点点
打在傘上
向我淺笑着
我是如何的希望

雨下着
永不止
路漫長
永不行完

78

The Long Hair

if you sometimes

think of our

those days

walking in the drizzle

raindrops tapping on

our umbrella

your smiling at me

how I wished

the drizzle

would never stop

the long path

would never end

湖上泛舟

春風自

堤岸楊柳

吹來

但願靜湖

為無際海洋

我们的小舟

遠遠離家门

80

rowing a boat

on the lake

spring breeze blowing

from the shore

of weeping willows

if the lake was

a boundless ocean

and our boat

far far from home

当妳在田野
　蹬跑时
背上一小包袋
　秋葉下落
我将轻扫
　妳的脸頰
妳笑着
将我向後束起来

when you are jogging

in the field

a light bag on you

autumn leaves falling

I shall softly

touch your cheek

as you laugh

tug me behind

在月光透过窗门
照入你的
房间
我會看著你
安靜的睡，
長夜
護衛妳

84

when the moonlight shines in

your bedroom

through the window

I shall watch you

sleep peacefully

will guard you safe

throughout the long night

也許一天
你的髮絲

遮蓋你的眼睛

沒有風吹

你可感到濕冷

及驚訝

你會想到

那是我嗎

perhaps someday

your long hair moves

covers your eyes

without any breeze

    would it astonish you

as you feel it wet and cool

    would you know

it was me

直至遥远的未来

一切皆过往

我们将在宇宙

不分离

採摘闪燦小宝石

乘坐小行星

追逐彗星

偵察遠方的信号

追踪神秘的光亮

观看新星的

出生

88

in the future when

everything becomes the past

we will be inseparable

in space

> *picking crystal stones*
>
> *riding on little asteroids*
>
> *chasing the comets*
>
> *tracing the distant signals*
>
> *following the mysterious lights*
>
> *watching the birth*
>
> > *of a star*

落下一光亮行星

一小女孩

向妳跑来

長髮飄蕩

相似妳

望着妳：

我以前見过妳嗎

拉着妳的手：

妳妳 我要带妳看

我的地方

landing on a lustrous planet

a little girl

running to you

long hair bouncing

resembling you

looking at you

"have I seen you before"

holding your hand

"I want to show you

my place"

到那一天
妳無意的回頭
看到妳的長髮
靜默的凝視妳
妳發覺原來
我一直衷心的
附着妳

淚滴下
妳緊握妳的長髮
低喚我的名字
我們繼續在
太空的歷程
追索深淵的智慧及
無窮的神奇事物

until one day

you turn around

you see your long hair

    silently gazing at you

you realize

it has been me loyally

    with you all the time

tears falling

you clutch your long hair

whisper my name

as we continue our adventures

    across the universe

pursuing wisdom

    and endless wonders

在一

遠方的銀河

二年經小生物

白一束在太空

浮过的長髮

揮着手

94

in a distant

    galaxy

two young beings

waving to a strand

of long hair in space

    passing by

我回身

遙遠的星星
抵家

我差不多

I was almost home

to my

home star

I turned back

97

通过云层

下落

她的金髮飘荡

咕噥声

盯视着我

淡水在她

闪烁的眼睛：

你不記得

我嗎

你從不跟我

說話

声音颤抖

消失雾靄中

98

descending

through the clouds

her golden hair waving

she stares at me

    muttering

tears in her

    glistening eyes

"do you not

    remember me

you never talked

    to me"

voice trembling

    vanished in the mist

我要时间停顿．

我不要
云朵浮遊

風吹噢

小溪暢流

海洋澎湃

I want the time to stop

I do not want

the clouds to move

the wind to blow

the brooks to flow

the oceans to roar

我要
下落的葉
止息在空中

密雨
房屋上不動

鳥兒在樹枝上
吱喳的叫

山崖的
瀑布

張開嘴合不攏

回轉激潑

I want

the leaves falling

to stay in the air

birds chirping

in the trees

with their beaks open

the rain coming down

pauses above the houses

the waterfalls

in the mountains

splashing upwards

我要整個世界

停下

靜止不動

在此時刻

104

I want the whole world

to stop

motionless

at this moment

地球將作
最後一次旋轉
不再有人類的
歷史 文化
星星瀏覽
不會醒來

月亮
告別的照耀
而遠去
長長的行程
往那境界
時間不存在

106

the earth will do

its last rotation

no more civilizations

    of mankind

stars will fall asleep

    will not awaken

the moon will shine

    one more time

leaving on an ultimate

    trip

to where

    there is no time

我要那

看到她的時刻

長留在我內裏

深深處

在世界的止動

宇宙的

寧靜當中

時鐘作

最後的滴答

時間不進

永恆的終結

I want the moment

seeing her

to stay with me

deep in me

in the stillness of the world

peacefulness

of the universe

as the clock

ticks its final tock

the time pauses

forever

我不要
多一天的生命

我不要醒來
看到陽光燦爛

我要這是
我最後的睡眠

I do not want

another day of my life

I do not want to wake up

to see the sun shining

I want this

my last sleep

我们将

生在一岩石

在太空通过

不同颜色的

间燥室石

在我们上面浮过

摘得一手满

她大声的欢笑

112

we shall be

riding on a rock

   going in space

shiny gemstones of

different colors

   floating above us

picking a handful

her loud laughter

月亮在那边

她遠遠的行程

揮着手：

「我希望她能

及時出宇宙」

此夜

我们最後一夜

114

the moon is out there

on her long journey

waving

"I hope she can be

out of the universe in time"

tonight

our last night

偎依著我：

你會記得我嗎

滑滑下：

你會有时

想想我嗎

擁著她

星星為我們一起

在我們後面

宇宙大限將至

安寧中

今夜

116

leaning on me

 "will you remember me"

tears falling

 "will you think of me

 once in a while"

holding her in my arms

stars with us

 behind us

the universe will end

 in peacefulness

tonight

looking back

as I leave

回望家園
低声告别

寒風
習習
烏雲湧至
我將整夜
號哭
直至我的淚
形成一河流
流動他去

wind blowing

furiously

dark clouds moving in rapidly

I shall cry

all night tonight

until my tears

form a river

flowing away

河　流

我將離去
不再聽到
妳的聲音
不看到妳的眼光
透入我心底處

122

The River

I shall be gone

     not anymore

hearing your voice

your eyes no longer

     penetrating me

別了妳

忘了妳

我將流去

志懷的地域

陽光下

青草在

和風中搖晃

春日百花

盛放

小鳥歡唱

跳躍

溪水

暢流

leaving you

forgetting you

    I shall go to the land

of oblivion

    under sunny sky

    green grass waving

in the breeze

    spring flowers

blossoming

    young birds singing

jumping

    creeks cheerfully

bubbling

流去

遠方的原野

高山静默

荒草摇曳

秋虫唧唧

天上寒星

好奇的

望下我

126

flowing into

    the far country

mountains asleep

    grass swaying

    insects chirping

stars in the cool sky

    curiously staring at me

below

没有妳的
回憶

没有失了妳的
心碎腸斷

我將流去
遠遠的

不復回

没有生命的心
空洞的身軀

讓那冰寒的
溪濤

沖裏我
掩蓋我

128

without the memories

of you

without the pain

of losing you

I shall flow away

as far as I can

to no return

a vacant body

a lifeless heart

with the chilly

roaring waves

crushing upon me

burying me

幾許光陰後

河流的声

終于低下來

緩緩的流

從而逐漸乾涸

河床上

積滿小石片

石塊

在天空

一浮云

洒下冷雨

靜靜的

圍繞着下面

乾涸了的

激烈淡河轉

130

until then

the sound of the river

diminishes

flowing slowly

and drying up

leaving at the banks

    pebbles

      rocks

    a cloud

      in the sky

shedding cool rain

quietly moving around

above the

dried river

    of raging tears

那是我旅程一生

的終結嗎

又或僅是

我冗長睡眠

的幻夢

was it the end

of my life journey

or did I just have

a dream of

    my life long sleep

向外望

昏暗一片

寂寂然

我在那裏

我是什么

我可存在

僅只我自己在

茫茫太虚嗎

我懼怕

我要喊

如一嬰兒喊叫

還下在太空中

134

looking out

an empty

vastness

where am I at

what am I

do I exist

am I alone

am I the only one here

so frightened

I want to cry

cry like a baby

left alone in space

我要尖喊

横越無声的空間

可有何人

何處

聽到我

發見我嗎

我做什么呢

何處去呢

何等孤零寂寞

如我能

跳回

我的睡眠

入我的長長夢境

再一次

没有明天

天天如是

136

I want to scream

across the silent space

if someones

      somewhere

can hear me

      spot me

without tomorrows

everyday is the same

what will I do

where will I go

how lonely I am

if only

I could fall back

in my sleep

to be in my long dream

      once again

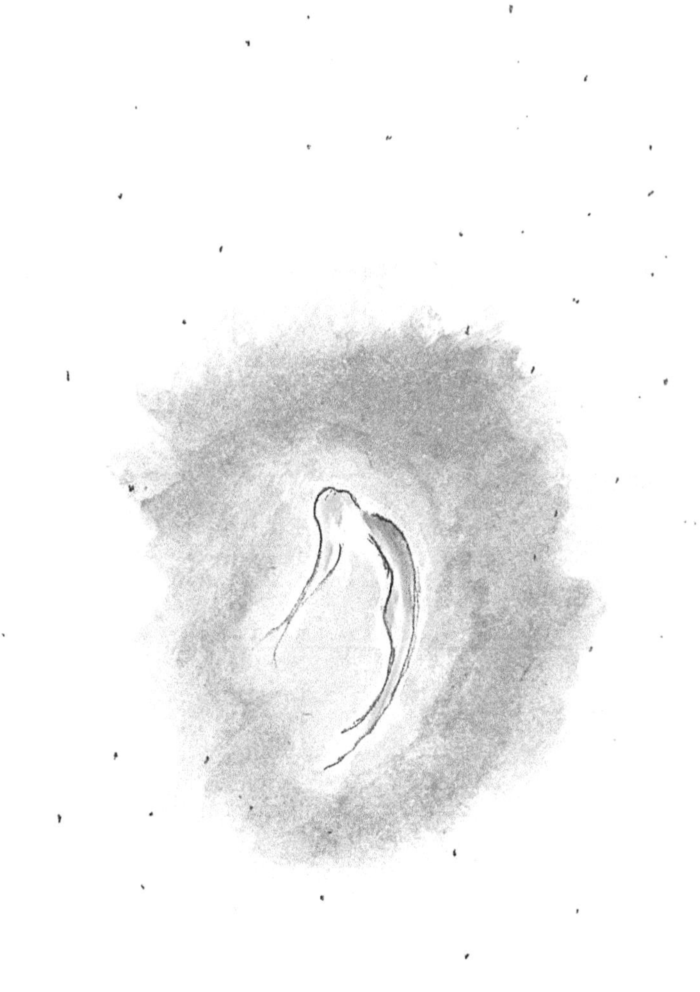

在寧靜的

宇宙

一小星

閃耀着

in the

peaceful universe

a tiny star

flickering

雪

每晚
臨睡時
我必然走至窗前
遙望天上的
星星
靜靜的
想着她

今夜
外面下雪
漫佈天際

142

Snow

every night

before I go to bed

I come to the window

looking up to the

distant stars

quietly

thinking of her

tonight

it snows

all over in the sky

每一白色的雪片
雅致的下落
尤如她
初春的鬱金香
溫和陽光中欢慶

湖畔堤岸的
青春垂柳
蕩漾在和風中
太空深淵處
百万年來
驟然到的火光

144

every piece of white snowflake

gracefully coming down

is the image of her

   an early spring tulip

rejoicing in the warm sunlight

   a young weeping willow

at the lake shore

swaying in the gentle breeze

   a gleaming light

from the deep universe

arriving in a million years

我喜欢雪夜

窗外

雪粉粉

我但愿是

树下一黄叶

风吹上

透过树枝

偷偷看她

脸热烘烘

心急速的跳

知道她正在外面

雪中

我便会安宁的

一直驰至天明

146

I like snowy nights

pieces of snow falling

outside my window

I would wish to be

the yellow leaf on the ground

going up in the wind

peeking at her

through the bare branches

my face burning

my heart pounding

knowing she is out there

in the snow

I would sleep peacefully

throughout the night

外面的雪

越下越大

雪片不斷打在

窗上

她正在這裏了

她遠遠到來

造訪我

向我揮手

顯示她手裏的

雪球

對着窗

擲向我

俏皮的笑

弄醒睡中的

樹上雪鳥

撲拍完的翅膀

盯着她

148

the snow is now
coming down heavily
    snowflakes are hitting
my windowpane
    she is here
she has come a long long way
to visit me
waving to me
    showing me a snowball
in her hand
    throwing it towards the window
at me
    laughing naughtily
awakening the snowy owl
on a tree
    it flaps its wings
stares at her

我要見她
　与她相會

開了窗門
　熄了燈

今夜
　我要提早上床睡覺

我將脱離
　我驅中的体魀

通过窗門
　飛出

直
上天空

150

I want to see her

    be with her

window opened

light turned off

    I shall go to bed early

tonight

    I shall leave my body

in sleep

    venture out

through the window

into the sky

星星在云後

憩息

夜沉沉

万籟俱寂

下面房屋燈暗

酣睡中

輕輕抹去她

臉上髮上的雪

凝視她

如一小星

別家外遊

在太空躍翔

152

stars resting

behind the clouds

the night is

deep and calm

houses dim

asleep below

softly wiping snow off

her face   her hair

gazing at her

a tiny star

away from home

leaping in space

落下她的雪球

雪片安宁的

牵着她的小手

飘下

望入她的眼睛

整个宇宙

与她雪中

雪粉粉下着

翩翩起舞

宛若我们独在

宇宙中

154

dropping her snowball

holding her little hand

    looking into her eyes

dancing with her

    in the snow

as if we are alone

    in the universe

snow peacefully

    falling

the whole universe is

snowing

窗帘

風吹起
我的睡衣濕潤
床上一白羽毛
外面陽光普照的早晨
窗框
雪水滴下

雪白新雪
滿鋪地面
雪鳥已不見
在樹上

curtains blowing

    in the wind

my pajamas wet

a white feather on my bed

a sunny morning outside

water dripping

    from the windowpane

fresh white snow

    covers the ground

the snowy owl is gone

    from he tree

「再會」

望向遠處

蔚藍天空

揮揮手

「謝謝你的

到來」

"good bye"

looking out to the

far blue sky

waving

"thank you

for coming"

每夜

我在窗前

望向

那遙遠的小星星

靜靜的閃爍着

every night

I stand by my window

looking to the

distant little star

   quietly twinkling

what is more happy

than when my daughter

calls me Dad

什么會使我
更快樂
过于我的女兒
叫我爸爸

山區路旁一長草

云塊在天空浮过
樹在風中摇動
我立在這裏
白天　黑夜
盼望
等待
有一朝
我们的汽車
在這路駛过

164

A long grass

on the mountain roadside

clouds moving above

    trees swaying in the wind

I stand here

    days and nights

waiting

    hoping

a car of ours

    drives by

someday

每当夕阳西下

倦鸟飞落地平线

夜风起

初雪到临时

我尤其思念

我的家

166

when the sun sets

tired birds fly down the horizon

evening wind blows

    or early snow arrives

I'll especially

    think of my home

我永遠記得那晚

我是如何的驚喜

護士手抱一嬰兒

向我走來：

是女孩

她是那么可愛

她有閃光的髮絲

明亮的眼睛

我從來見過

她望出窗外：

天空有奇異的彩光

閃耀著

168

I always remember the night

how thrilled I was

the nurse came up to me

a baby in her arms

"it is a girl

she is such a darling

she has shiny hair

brilliant eyes

I have never seen before"

looking out the window

"there were strange lights

flashing in the sky"

那彷如
我的小女兒
張開她的眼睛
第一次
四周觀看她的世界
停在我面前：
「爸爸」
甜蜜的笑容
在她的小臉上
回復睡覺

170

it was as though

my little daughter

opened her eyes

looked around her world

for the first time

paused at me

    "hi Dad"

a sweet smile

on her tiny face

went back to sleep

而我在這裏望向
那些車
一架跟一架
如我能看到我们的家車
夹着我们孩兒
喜乐融融的欢笑声
再一次
在這路经过

172

and here I look out

to the cars

one after another

  if one day I can see ours

with the laughter and joy

of our children

coming down this road

once again

夜幕下垂

最後的一車已過

在我心底裏

我所期待的一天

將永不到來

每次我看到

別人快樂的家車

駛過時

我黯然

垂下

when dusk approaches

the last car has gone by

deep in me

I know our car

> *will never come*

every time I see

other happy family cars

> *pass by*

I sadly

> *bow down*

上面的月光
时常沉静
柔和银光
泻在大地
树叶片片下落
远处传来
山狼咆哮声

明早是一
新希望
黎明曙光
射过高山时

the moon up there

always stoic

silvery moonlight gently

touching the ground

leaves falling

howls of wolves

   from a distance

a new hope

in the morning

when the first rays of dawn

peek over the mountains

一天尤如

我们伟大的宇宙

变更完的道程

我聽見

自遠遠来

孩兒欢乐的笑声

我抬頭

看到一輛車慢慢地

朝着我處来

停下

一小女孩

步出車门

如一小天使

自天上下来

她髮上

有一紫色丝带

伺着我走来

178

one day

as if our mighty universe

    has altered its course

I heard the laughing voices

    of children

        from a distance

rising up

I see a car

    slowly approaching

it stops

a little girl

    gets out of the car

like a little angel

    from heaven

she has a purple ribbon

    in her hair

walking towards me

在這世上

還會誰呢

那是我的小女兒

我時常懷念

白天 晚上

醒着 睡着

我驚喜不已

難以相信

在我眼前的

我在夢中嗎

我不在這世界了嗎

180

who else in the world

could she be

that is my little daughter

whom I think of

day and night

awake or asleep

I exclaim

I cannot believe

what I saw

am I dreaming

am I in another world

我的女兒長高了

那么漂亮

可愛

我恨不得跳出去

緊抱她在我懷裏

不再讓她

離開我

my daughter is growing

so pretty

so adorable

I want to jump out

hold her in my arms

will not let her

leave me anymore

她行近

無限親情的望著我：

媽

這長草

那么的虛弱及憔悴

它在這裏豈不太冷嗎

我覺得它很熟悉的

有水点滴下

它在流淚

它在向我搖擺

我聽到它叫我

它知道我的名字呢

妳聽見嗎 媽

它要我行近些

它有話要跟我說

184

she comes close

gazes at me

"Mom

this long grass looks

so weak and pale

isn't it too cold here

I feel I knew it before

there is water dripping

it is crying

it is swaying at me

I heard it call me

it knows my name

did you hear Mom

it is asking me to come closer

it wants to talk to me"

「我的小孩兒

妳終于來了

媽媽聽不到我的

妳可知道

爸爸如何的掛念妳

想着妳

等待這一天到來」

186

"my little daughter

you finally came

    Mom could not hear me

do you know

    how much Dad missed you

    thought of you

waited for this day to come"

「爸爸在這裏很好

妳有一顆很善良

柔和的心

我很安慰

爸爸很難過

未曾

做到我對家庭的

責任

未曾照顧妳

好使妳有個

十分快樂的童年」

"Daddy is fine here

you have a very kind

   and tender heart

I am very pleased

Daddy is so sorry

   has not been able

to do my duties

   for the family

and to take care of you

   to provide you

a very happy childhood"

「爹地將看不到妳

逐漸長大

看不到妳

放學回家

將書包拋在

沙發上：

「媽我很餓」

190

"Daddy will miss seeing yiou

    grow up

will not see you

    coming home from school

throwing your bag

    on the couch:

    Mom I am hungry"

「將不能

在家庭旅遊

上高山

看妳跪低

手餵金花鼠

溪河

綑小魚

勿妳的小羊羣

競奔上山崖

向遠

拋擲小石塊

」

192

"will not be able to take you

on a family trip

to the mountains

to see you kneel down

feeding a chipmunk

netting little fish

at the creek

racing your brother

to the cliff

throwing little stones

over the edge"

在那天
妳穿上白莎服
手上
美麗鮮花束
爸爸將不能
牽著妳的手
微笑著
驕傲地
行下妳的婚礼大堂

唯有在這裏
望上碧天
默默祝福我的女兒
美滿
幸福的生活
」

194

"on the day

you wear a white gown

clutch a bouquet of beautiful flowers

in her hands

Daddy will not be able

to hold your hand

smilingly

proudly

walking you down the wedding aisle

but out here

looking up at the sky

wishing my daughter

a happy

wonderful life"

「爹吔很榮幸高興
　作為妳的父親

在妳選擇
　我们的家而下來

勤力讀書
　長大為一

聰慧偉大的女人
　從妳第一天的

生命

当妳將閉妳的眼睛
　望着爹吔時

我便知道妳是真正
　爹吔的女兒

我已知道妳不會
　久留在这世界

他日
　妳會離去」

196

"Daddy is so happy and fortunate
to be your father
that you chose to come
to our family
     study well
grow up to be
a wise and great woman
     from the first day
of your life
when you opened your eyes
and looked at Daddy
I knew you were truly
Daddy's daughter
I knew you won't be
     here very long
someday
     you will leave"

「好好照顧媽媽

及小弟弟

我全要依靠妳了

為我們的家庭

那麼多的義務

責任

那麼沉重的負担

落在一女孩身上

爸爸要哭了

妳會代爸爸做到嗎

我的小女兒

妳會原諒爸爸嗎」

198

"take care of Mom

and your young brother

    I will have to rely on you

for our family

    so many responsibilities

duties

    such a heavy burden

on a little girl

    Daddy wants to cry

    will you do it for Daddy

      my daughter

    will you forgive Daddy"

「在那一天的到來

我會在海洋裏

廣潤藍天

浪浪捲動

清風吹拂

晚上

凡星閃爍

我不會寂寞的

我尚有件事未了

要靜心的做

我知道妳明白我

妳是我的女兒啊」

"I will be at the ocean

      someday

wide blue sky

waves rolling

wind blowing

      stars

        twinkling

I won't be lonely

I still have some work

      to do quietly

I know you understand me

      you are my daughter"

她泪珠莹莹

点点头

点点头

若如她应允及

明白她的父亲

、她的小手

小心翼翼地抹去

长草上的水珠

202

her eyes brim with tears

she nods

nods

like she promises and

understands her father

her little hand

carefully wipes the water drops

on the long grass

「我不要你獨自一人

在這裏　爸爸

我要你回家

我要你為我放

那你做給我的

風箏上天空

我要你帶我去攀登

爾卑斯雪嶺

你答應過我的　爸爸
」

"I don't want you

to be alone here Dad

I want you to come home

so we can fly the kite

you made for me

into the sky

I want you to take me

to the Alps

like you promised me Dad"

「我要向那雪鳥

雪女孩是否很漂亮

它可否知道

她來自

那一顆星星

我要走上雪峯頂：

她會否重回

一百万年後」

206

"I want to ask the snowy owl

if the snow girl is pretty

if it knows which star

she came from

I want to climb to

the summit:

will she return

in a million years"

「請回家 爸爸

何可知道每晚

餐桌前 你不在

我們是如何的感受

你知道嗎

媽常離桌

偷偷抹眼淚
」

她除下她髮上的

紫色絲帶

小心地束在

長草上：

「我永遠與你一起的爸爸

不論將來我在何處

爸爸

我是你的小女兒
」

"please come home Dad

do you know how we feel

at the dinner table every night

without you

do you know

Mom always walks away

quietly wipes her eyes"

she pulls the purple ribbon

from her hair

carefully ties it around

the long grass

"I am always with you

wherever I go to

Dad

I am your daughter"

抹着眼：

我會在

宇宙呼嘯

我有个

地球爸爸

wiping her eyes

"I will shout out

in the universe

I have an

Earth father"

她的母親走上

望望那長草

牽著她女兒的手

行開去

女兒回頭望

看到她的父親

一瞬間

變得那么蒼老

無依靠

在寒風中動搖

她再也忍不住

她的淚

奪眶而出

她掙脫出

她母親的手握

哇的一声大叫

212

her mother comes up

looks at the long grass

takes her daughter's hand

ushers her away

the daughter looks back

sees her father

all of a sudden

becomes so old

helpless

bending in the cold wind

she cannot hold her tears

any longer

bursting out

she breaks away from

her mother's grasp

cries loudly

手掩面

走向那部車：

「為什么這樣無情

對待我爸爸

我不會放过這的

我要我爸爸

我要我爸爸」

214

her hands over her eyes

running to the car

"why it is so cruel

to my Dad

I will not tolerate it

I want my Dad

I want my Dad"

从她眼裏

涌下的泪

可形成一小河

花她父亲的河流

身旁

一起流动他去

夹着她大声的

欢呼声

216

the tears

streaming down her eyes

can form a little river

by the side of

her father's river

flowing away together

with her

loud laughing voice

在天空

明耀的光線

透过云层射出

in the sky

lights bursting out

through the clouds

車子慢慢的離去

消逝在我淡水

朦朧的眼睛

風呼喚

樹葉吹起

山路回復原來的

空無

冷清

220

the car slowly recedes

disappears from my eyes

   welled with tears

wind blowing

leaves floating

the mountain roadside

is empty

   and silent once again

俱往矣
一切已成过去

我能再见到
我的女儿吗

宇宙已经为
我的女儿改变

遵程一次
我岂能有

再多的新望

it is all gone

all over

will I ever be able

to see my daughter again

the universe has already

altered its course once

for my daughter

can I expect

another one

我忽然感到

那么孤零

从所未有的

寂寞

如一空洞的樹幹

漂泊在

浩瀚海洋中

不知

何所去

224

I suddenly feel alone

so lonely

I ever did

I do not know

where to go

like a hollow tree trunk

floating

on the ocean

endlessly

我感到很舒適

平靜

我要做的已做到

長久心願已達

我已見到我的女兒

我有短暫的幸福時刻

看我的女兒在一起

我的女兒叫我爸爸

我的女兒寬恕了

她的父親

I feel relaxed

    peaceful

my task accomplished

my wish fulfilled

I have seen my daughter

I had some great moments

    with my daughter

my daughter called me Dad

my daughter has forgiven

    her Dad

我從不知道

作為一個孩的父親

原來是那么的美好

為何我等了那么久

才來這世上呢

我對我的一生

可有抱怨嗎

我已得到我

額外应得的

228

I never realized

how wonderful it is to be

a girl's father

why did I wait so long

to come to this world

do I have any complaints

of my life

I have received much more

than I deserve

我仍能留在此地
烘熱太陽下

徹骨寒風
冷雨

雪霜
無期了的傷痛

哀愁的回憶嗎

230

Can I still be here

under the burning sun

in the bone chilling wind

freezing rain

icy sleets

with the memories of

endless pain and sorrow

向上望

白云悠悠的在

趕程

也許這該是我

離去的時候了

帶着我女兒給我的

紫色絲帶

向上去

加入白云的行列

looking up

the clouds are moving hastily

on their journeys

it is probably time

for me to leave

carrying the purple ribbon

my daughter gave me

going up

joining the clouds

纖弱的月亮

陰鬱

昏瞆
此夕

將不亮照
掛在清寒的

夜空
靜默不動

234

the delicate moon

gloomy

dim

will not want to shine

this evening

hanging in the

cool sky

motionless

也許沒注意到

我在云裏

浮過

今夜將看不到

我在下面

地上一空洞

山草搖曳

樹影不定

秋虫瑟縮鳴叫

一陣冷風抹過

荒涼的山路

樹葉沙沙響

236

may have not noticed me
in the cloud
passing by
will not see me there
tonight
an empty spot on the ground
grass swaying
moving shadows of trees
sounds of shivering insects
a sweep of chilly wind
over the desolate road
leaves rustling

237

風長嘯

一幽声在細雨中：

我以為我已

給来了我的行程

留不在

遠岸宙裏

望向消失中的云塊：

我知道我不會

再見到你

238

wind whistling

a voice in the rain

"I thought I would

finish my journey here

and stay in

this universe"

looking to the diminishing cloud

"I know I won't

see you again

但我不會忘記
　那許多在
上邊的長夜
我從不敢問你
　可要
陪我一起同去

一滴淚下：
　我知道
你不會

240

but I won't forget

those long nights

at the mountain

    I have never dared to ask

if you would want

to go with me"

    a tear shedding

"I knew

    you wouldn't"

「我有些疲倦

但我會離去

我不能在此

多留一晚

还有多少个宇宙

我會经过

逃过

我會邂逅到什么呢

可有高点吗」

242

"I am a little tired

but I will leave

I can't stay here

for another night

how many more universes

will I pass by

or go through

what will I then encounter

will there be any mountains"

「我的行程

會無期盡嗎

我會抵我

最終目的地嗎

那裏

時間不存在

那是什麼樣的

我又如何永久的

活下去呢

」

244

"will my journey

ever end

will I ever arrive

my final destination

where time

does not exist

what will it be like

when I live my life

without end"

「我不要想下去

我很怕

你想到那處呢

你想念你的地球嗎

你會否知道

看到我　在哭嗎」

相逢　訣別

如一流星的未

流星的去

此宵何堪

月圓　月完

我的命

不是早已

注定了嗎

長空蕭然

前路茫茫

來日悠悠

無了期

我如何

消受下去

246

"I dont want to think about it

I am scared

where are you now

do you miss your Earth

do you know

do you see

I am crying"

無声的離去
隻身如來時一樣
沒有人認識我
記得我
不留下一然痕跡
如我
從不曾到來
不曾存在

248

leaving quietly

alone as I came

no one to know me

    to remember me

no trace left of me

    as if

I have never been here

    never existed

向下望

最後一鳥兒

飛下歸家

煙霧自我家煙囪

冒出

黃葉落下

後園

兩小草車

靠在圍欄

一梯子倚在

蘋菓樹上

戶外餐枱

有四椅子

淚滴下：

教我如何能

留下我的家

而去呢

250

looking below

the last bird

flying home

smoke rising

from our house chimney

yellow leaves falling

on our yard

two small bikes

by the fence

a ladder

leans on the apple tree

a patio table

with four chairs

tears falling

"how can I depart

leaving my family

behind"

不论过往的生命

欢乐或哀伤

皆如我家里

烟囱的烟

上升

消逝于天空里

如从不曾存在

252

whatever one's life has been

joyous or sorrowful

it was like the smoke

　　　rising from

our house chimney

　　　vanished into the sky

like it has never been there

再會

也許我们會再相逢
不知的地方
冥冥的未來
誰知道呢
或許不會
也或許我们
在隔路走过

妳向我一瞥：
我以前見过
這人嗎
為何我同裏
在起伏呢
回頭望陌路人
在妳走妳的
而我惆然
走我的

goodbye

maybe we will meet again

somewhere

beyond time

who knows

or we may not

or else we may

pass each other's path

you catch a glimpse of me

"had I known

this person before

why it is beating

within me"

looking back at me

as you go on your way

and I go

on mine

对那些曾疼伤过我的

那些我伤害过的

早已忘记过往

我希望能倒转

那曾为我流溅的

我可没有不注意到

那许多昆虫

在我一生脚踏过

及那数不尽的陆地

及水裏生物

曾支持我的生命

而生存

我十分不忍

极之难过

但望牠们

永远安息

256

to those who had harmed me

it was all long gone and forgotten

to those I had hurt

I wish it could have been reversed

to the ones who had wept for me

it did not go unnoticed

to the many insects

I stepped on in my life time

and the numerous land

and water lives

that have supported

my life to live

I am very very sorry

deeply sorry

I wish they

rest peacefully

多么的懊悔

多深的

肉痛

如若我不曾

有生命

或不曾到此世界

但只

一塵埃

徘徊在

太空裏

so much remorse

so much grief

    within me

if I never

    had a life or never

        came to the world

but merely

a dot of dust

hovering

    in massive space

没有说再會
没有回頭顧
黯然的在
云裏離去

我聽到一陣
哭泣声嗎
在渺茫
那裏
寂靜的宇宙
未的呢

星星靜靜的
閃爍著

260

without goodbye

    without glancing back

leaving quietly

    in the cloud

did I hear someone

    sobbing

where in the tranquil universe

    did it come from

stars are calmly

    twinkling

至一遠遠的星系
一幻像
那難忘的家居
出現

煙霧上升
雀鳥在雲中
雨小孩兒在風中
樹旁遊玩
一喜悅歡笑声
向着我奔来

262

into a far galaxy

a vision of

an unforgettable house

    appearing

smoke rising from the chimney

birds in the clouds

two children playing

    by the trees in the wind

a joyous voice

    running towards me

幻像

模糊消失

逝去寧靜中

点点冷雨

自太空

落下

下

向宇宙的

深底處去

264

the vision

    diminishing

vanished in silence

drops of cool rain

    falling from space

down

    down

to the bottom of

the universe

如有一天

我能追上
那石塊

出宇宙
到那

淵外之外

if one day

    I can catch up

to the stone

out of the universe

    to the

beyond

直至那时
生命已过往

星星不再现
而在那空无

无声的太空
一光亮的车辆

缓缓驶出
附着那熟悉

孩儿的
嘻哈欢乐声

268

until the time

no life

   no stars

in the vacuous

   noiseless universe

an illuminated image of a car

   emerging

with the acquainted

   cheerful laughter voices

of children

不論宇宙的定數

何時到來

就讓那部出現的

家庭車

為宇宙的

過程及歷史

最後一次跡象吧

從此宇宙在

沒有再多騷擾下

將合上眼

安寧的睡眠

永恆地

whenever the destiny

of our universe comes

may the occurance of

that happy family car

be the final event

in the duration and history

of the universe

and the universe

without any further disturbances

will then fall asleep

in peace

eternally

也許下一回

在靜默深淵的宇宙
　一線微光

慢慢的冒出

誰是那女兒
多些關于
那女兒的事蹟
　將在
紫色絲帶
二集

272

maybe another time

    in the empty

deep space

a beam of light

    slowly

piercing out

Who is the daughter
more about the daughter
will be in
The Purple Ribbon II

Gazing at me
    "will you remember me"
tears welled in her eyes
    "will you think of me
        once in a while"

Stars with us
    behind us
the universe will end
    in peacefulness
        tonight

望著我：
你會記得我嗎
淚水滿溢她的眼眶：
你會偶爾
想想我嗎

星星與我們一起
在我們後面
宇宙大限將至
寧靜中
今夜

Lightning Source UK Ltd.
Milton Keynes UK
UKHW020445261120
374084UK00001B/18